A HARRY PO
QUIZ FOR MUGGLES:

BONUS SPELLS, FACTS & TRIVIA

BY

SEBASTIAN CARPENTER

Eaglestar Books

First published by Eaglestar Books, 2020

This Continental Edition first issued by Eaglestar Books in paperback and digital edition

Printed in Great Britain

Eaglestar Books

PO Box 7086

Harrow, London

HA2 5WN, United Kingdom

Also, in the series…

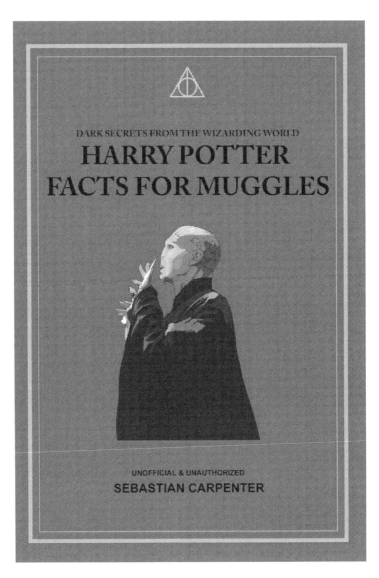

Don't miss out on the #1 New Release and Part Two in the series: *Harry Potter Facts For Muggles.*

TABLE OF CONTENTS

Preface

The first of the *Harry Potter* books was published the same year that the final Battle of Hogwarts took place. J.K. Rowling declared that "I open at the close".

Rowling first came up with idea for *Harry Potter* while she was delayed on a train from Manchester to London's King's Cross Station back in 1990.

The first book *Harry Potter and the Philosopher's Stone* is based on a young boy who on his eleventh birthday, discovers he has magical powers and that he is "The Boy Who Lived" following the murder of his wizard parents by "He Who Must Not Be Named".

Skip forward to the present day and well over two decades later that brave and remarkable wizard has become a household name around the globe. The success of the books speak for themselves having sold 50 million copies worldwide making it the best-selling series in history.

These historic novels captured the minds of kids and adults alike, sparking the manifestation of a dream of how life would be to live in a fantasy wizarding world. And they were the inspiration that catapulted the creation of this trip down memory lane and unearthing of new *Harry Potter* facts in the form of an exciting trivia publication.

With that being said folks, Happy Quizarding and remember "The stories we love best, live in us forever".

Trivia Score Honour Roll – Which Wizard Are You?

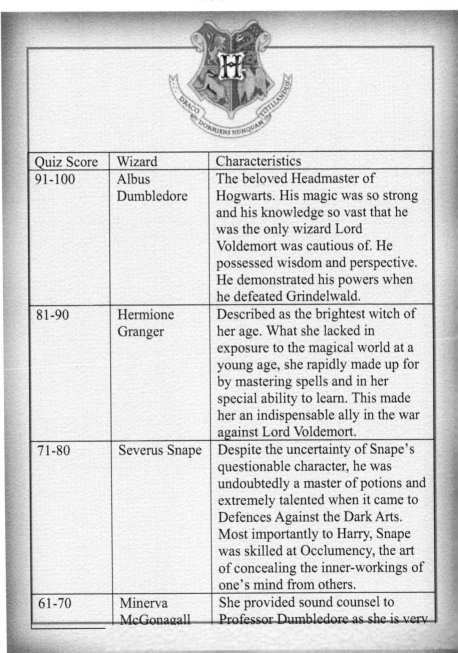

Quiz Score	Wizard	Characteristics
91-100	Albus Dumbledore	The beloved Headmaster of Hogwarts. His magic was so strong and his knowledge so vast that he was the only wizard Lord Voldemort was cautious of. He possessed wisdom and perspective. He demonstrated his powers when he defeated Grindelwald.
81-90	Hermione Granger	Described as the brightest witch of her age. What she lacked in exposure to the magical world at a young age, she rapidly made up for by mastering spells and in her special ability to learn. This made her an indispensable ally in the war against Lord Voldemort.
71-80	Severus Snape	Despite the uncertainty of Snape's questionable character, he was undoubtedly a master of potions and extremely talented when it came to Defences Against the Dark Arts. Most importantly to Harry, Snape was skilled at Occlumency, the art of concealing the inner-workings of one's mind from others.
61-70	Minerva McGonagall	She provided sound counsel to Professor Dumbledore as she is very

		worldly and full of wisdom. She was one of very few registered Animagi. She too became Hogwarts' Headmistress, and she was once able to hold her own in a duel against Voldemort for a while.
51-60	Harry Potter	Harry is the protagonist of the story, but this admirably doesn't make him the know-it-all of the wizarding world. He excelled in potions and Defence Against the Dark Arts. His courage was unquestionable, but his ability to learn fast and adapt to situations ultimately led to his survival.

41-50	Sirius Black	Sirius was charismatic and a top student during his time at Hogwarts, despite a lack of effort when it came to studying. He became an Animagus at a young age and proved to be a remarkable strategist by escaping from the clutches of Azkaban Prison and its dreaded guards, the Dementors.
31-40	Lily Potter	Her fate was a tragic end at the hands of Lord Voldemort. But before this she had demonstrated incredible magical abilities from a young age. She was born into a muggle family, yet her talents shone in potions, charms and transfiguration. She was also part of the Slug Club, which of course, only the top students get to partake in.
21-30	Remus Lupin	Lupin is widely known for being a werewolf, and he definitely let this effect his confidence. He was very mature and a worthy confident to Harry. He was also very skilled when it came to Defence Against the Dark Arts and had a knack for teaching his students crucial skills in this area.
11-20	Fred & George Weasley	Fred and George were never model students, that is true. However, they proved throughout the series that they were the most resourceful and entrepreneurial characters. They invented numerous magical objects and they opened a joke shop which was a thriving establishment in Diagon

0-10	Ron Weasley	Ron eventually became an Auror and went on to reform and revolutionise the Ministry of Magic. He was loyal and very determined on his mission to aid Harry and Hermione.

Chapter 1: Muggle Level Quiz Questions

Muggle Level Questions 1-15:

1. When is Harry Potter's birthday?

2. Who guards the entrance to the Gryffindor common room?

3. What profession do Hermione Grainger's parents do for a living?

4. There is a bright green snake that guards the Chamber of Secrets, what is it called?

5. What is Lord Voldemort's real name?

6. Harry plays in which position for the Gryffindor Quidditch Team?

7. What is the name given to Lord Voldemort's most ardent followers?

8. Out of which platform does the Hogwarts Express depart from at London's King Cross Station?

9. What does Albus Dumbledore use to light up the street of Privet Drive?

10. Hagrid's pet dragon is which species?

11. Name the Deputy Headmistress of Hogwarts and the Head of Gryffindor House?

12. Who is the Defence Against the Dark Arts teacher in *Harry Potter and the Order of the Phoenix*?

13. What is the address that Harry lives at with his aunt and uncle?

14. Which little picturesque location is the only all-wizarding

village in Britain?

15.   What name is given to the deadly phantoms that guard
       Azkaban Prison?

FIND THE ANSWERS
ON THE
NEXT PAGE!

Muggle Level Answers 1-15

1. July 31.
2. The Fat Lady.
3. Dentists.
4. A basilisk.
5. Tom Marvolo Riddle.
6. Seeker.
7. Death Eaters.
8. Platform 9 ¾.
9. Put-Outer (Deluminator)
10. Norwegian Ridgeback.
11. Professor Minerva McGonagall.
12. Delores Umbridge.
13. Number 4, Privet Drive, Little Whinging.
14. Hogsmeade.
15. Dementors.

Muggle Level Questions 16-30:

16. What language can snakes and serpents speak?

17. How did Harry get the scar on his forehead?

18. Who kills Professor Dumbledore?

19. What does the Mirror of Erised do?

20. How are the students of Hogwarts placed into their house?

21. What is the name of Fred and George's joke shop?

22. Who is the ghost of Hufflepuff?

23. What is the name of Harry's beloved snowy owl?

24. How does Harry breathe underwater during the second task of the Tri-Wizard Tournament?

25. Who is Fluffy?

26. "You're a little scary sometimes, you know that? Brilliant... but scary." Who is Ron giving this awkward compliment to?

27. What object must be caught in order to end a Quidditch match?

28. In *Harry Potter & the Order of the Phoenix*, what colour is Tonks' hair when we first meet her?

29. "The ones who love us never really leave us." Who says this and which movie is it from?

30. What is Rita Skeeter known for?

FIND THE ANSWERS ON THE NEXT PAGE!

Muggle Level Answers 16-30

16. Parseltongue.
17. Harry got the scar when Voldemort tried to kill him as a baby.
18. Severus Snape, a former Death-Eater, kills Dumbledore with the "Avada Kedavra" killing curse.
19. It shows the desire of your heart. Dumbledore states to Harry that the mirror of Erised "shows us nothing more or less than the deepest, most desperate desire of our hearts".
20. First year students are assigned their houses by placing the sorting hat on their heads.
21. Weasley's Wizard Wheezes.
22. The Fat Friar.
23. Hedwig.
24. He eats gillyweed.
25. A dog with three heads who was once cared for by Hargid. Fluffy's greatest weakness was that he was unable to resist falling asleep to the sound of music.
26. Hermione.
27. The Golden Snitch,.
28. Purple.
29. Sirius Black in *Harry Potter and the Prisoner of Azkaban*.
30. Rita Skeeter is known for being a witch journalist for the *Daily Prophet*.

Muggle Level Questions 31-50:

31. What are the names of Ron Weasley's parents?

32. Which character owned a Firebolt broomstick?

33. What is the name of the magical map of Hogwarts?

34. Argus Filch's pet cat is named what?

35. Located in London, what is the name of the bustling shopping area that magic folk visit?

36. What is the name of the Ghost that resides in the Gryffindor Tower?

37. There is only one bank in the wizarding world, what is it called?

38. Who does Harry marry?

39. What is the name of the secret society that Albus Dumbledore founded?

40. In what year was the first *Harry Potter* movie released?

41. Where is the Slytherin common room located?

42. Who played Lord Voldemort in the *Harry Potter* movies?

43. What is Professor Flitwick's first name?

44. Where did Harry Potter train Dumbledore's army?

45. Who is Albus Dumbledore's brother?

46. Bellatrix Lestrange was killed by whom?

47. How did Harry catch his first snitch?

48.   What is the name of Albus Dumbledore's phoenix companion and defender?

49.   How did Moaning Myrtle die?

50.   What match did Harry watch at the Quidditch World Cup

FIND THE ANSWERS ON THE NEXT PAGE!

Muggle Level Answers 31-50

31. Molly and Arthur Weasley.
32. Harry was given the Firebolt broomstick at the end of the third book by Sirius.
33. The Marauder's Map. The map was created by Messrs. Moony, Wormtail, Padfoot, and Prongs.
34. Mrs. Norris. The cat alerts Filch to any student mischief inside the school grounds.
35. Diagon Alley is the wizarding shopping street situated behind the Leaky Cauldron in central London.
36. Nearly Headless Nick.
37. Gringotts Wizarding Bank. It is owned and run by goblins.
38. Harry married Ginny Weasley. They eventually had three kids together: James Sirius, Albus Severus and Lily Luna Potter.
39. The Order of the Phoenix.
40. *Harry Potter and the Philosopher's Stone* was released in 2001. It was directed by Chris Columbus.
41. The dungeons.
42. Actor Ralph Fiennes played Lord Voldemort in the movie franchise.
43. Filius.
44. The Room of Requirement. This is a magical room that will only appear when someone is in great need and it will be equipped with the seeker's needs.
45. Aberforth Dumbledore.
46. Molly Weasley.
47. Harry accidentally "caught" his first Golden Snitch in his mouth.
48. Fawkes.
49. Myrtle darted into the girls bathroom to hide from Olive Hornby after she teased her about her glasses. At that time she heard someone come into the bathroom (the basilisk). She later died after directly looking into the eyes of the basilisk.
50. Harry watched Bulgaria play Ireland at the Quidditch World Cup.

Muggle Level Questions 51-65:

51. What symbol represents the Gryffindor house?

52. Who accompanied Harry to the Yule Ball?

53. In the film adaptation of *Harry Potter and the Chamber of Secrets,* what does Draco Malfoy call Hermione to insult her?

54. Who is Peeves?

55. What type of Dragon did Harry face in his first Tri-Wizard Tournament task?

56. After seeing a Dementor, what can make a person feel better?

57. When Dumbledore and Harry first visit Horace Slughorn, what is he disguised as?

58. Who was the headmaster of Hogwarts before Professor Dumbledore?

59. Gilderoy Lockhart accidentally casts a spell on himself in *Harry Potter and the Chamber of Secrets.* What spell did he use?

60. What custom do wizard folk undertake before a duel?

61. Which famous and calming lake is situated south of the Hogwarts Castle?

62. The mythical centaur is an amalgamation of which two animals?

63. What is the name of the student of Hogwarts who commented on the school's Quidditch contests?

64. Who founded Hogwarts School of Witchcraft and Wizardry?

65. What colour are Harry Potter's eyes?

FIND THE ANSWERS
ON THE
NEXT PAGE!

Muggle Level Answers 51-65

51. Gryffindor values courage, and therefore its symbol is the lion.
52. Harry took Parvati Patil to the Yule Ball.
53. A "filthy little mudblood".
54. Peeves was a poltergeist at Hogwarts. He was particularly fond of mischief and chaos often driving Argus Filch up the wall.
55. Harry faced a Hungarian Horntail.
56. Chocolate. Eating chocolate after seeing a dementor releases endorphins into the body which boosts one's mood.
57. Dumbledore, accompanied by Harry found Slughorn disguised as an armchair in a muggle village called Budleigh Babberton.
58. Armando Dippet.
59. "Obliterate". This backfired following an attempt to alter Ron Weasley's memory using a faulty wand.
60. They face each other and bow.
61. The Great Lake or Black Lake.
62. A centaur is a fictional half-man, half-horse beast.
63. Lee Jordan.
64. There were four founders: Rowena Ravenclaw, Helga Hufflepuff, Godric Gryffindor and Salazar Slytherin.
65. Green.

Muggle Level Questions 66-80:

66.   In which prison was Gellert Grindelwald locked up inside?

67.   What did Lucius Malfoy unintentionally give to Dobby to set him free?

68.   Madame Maxine is the headmistress of which academy?

69.   What person would be able to release the seal on the Chamber of Secrets?

70.   What gift does Mrs. Weasley present Harry with every year?

71.   Where do wizard kind get their news from?

72.   What is a horcrux?

73.   Albus Dumbledore is entombed with which magical object?

74.   Why does Severus Snape vow to protect Harry?

75.   Who won the 1994 Quidditch World Cup?

76.   Viktor Krum attended which school?

77.   What is the name of the mysterious area of land situated to the west of Hogwarts?

78.   What club was formed by Horace Slughorn as an opportunity to host his most favoured students?

79.   A witch or wizard who can mutate into an animal when so desired is known as a what?

80.   Oliver Wood went on to play for which professional Quidditch team?

FIND THE ANSWERS ON THE NEXT PAGE!

66. The Prison of Nurmengard located in Austria.
67. Harry's dirty sock.
68. Beauxbatons Academy of Magic.
69. The Heir of Slytherin.
70. A new sweater.
71. The *Daily Prophet*, their main office is located in London, England.
72. An object containing a part of someone's soul. In order to create a horcrux, one must commit murder.
73. He is buried with the Elder Wand, the most powerful wand of them all.
74. He was in love with Harry's mother, Lily Potter.
75. The Irish beat the Bulgarians to triumph during the 1994 Quidditch World Cup.
76. Durmstrang Institute. The school as a suspect reputation when it comes to teaching the Dark Arts.
77. The Forbidden Forest. It is named as such because of the dangerous creatures that reside there, such as the acromantulas.
78. The Slug Club.
79. Animagus.
80. He played as a reserve for Puddlemere United, presumably as a keeper.

Muggle Level Questions 81-100:

81. Which illegal curse gives someone the ability to control another?

82. What is the name of the occupation given to someone who is trained to catch dark wizards?

83. How did the Weasley's rescue Harry from the Dursley's before the start of the second year?

84. How does Fawkes the phoenix heal Harry's wound after he's bitten by the basilisk?

85. Who did Peter Pettigrew, an animagus, turn himself into after the worst betrayal imaginable?

86. Who were the two representatives of Hogwarts School to compete in the Tri-Wizard tournament?

87. How was Hermione able to take extra lessons during her third year?

88. What patronus can Harry cast?

89. Who referred to Ron as "Won-Won" during their spell dating?

90. Which character turns into a beetle to spy on goings on at Hogwarts?

91. After the death of Aragog, who collects valuable venom from him?

92. Professor McGonagall teachers what?

93. Which professor was concealing Lord Voldemort under his turban at the end of the *Philosopher's Stone*?

94. There is one book in the *Harry Potter* series that doesn't feature Lord Voldemort, which one is it?

95. Which word was added to the Oxford English Dictionary back in 2003?

96. Can you list the order of Weasley siblings in the correct order starting from the oldest to the youngest?

97. Hermione can manifest what patronus?

98. What is Professor Dumbledore's full name?

99. There are three unforgivable curses, what are they?

100. What is the name of the graveyard where Lord Voldemort murdered Cedric Diggory?

FIND THE ANSWERS ON THE NEXT PAGE!

Muggle Level Answers 81-100

81. The Imperius Curse.
82. Auror.
83. In a flying Ford Anglia car.
84. Fawkes cries on Harry's and the tears heal him.
85. Scabbers the Rat. He morphed after his betrayal of James and Lily Potter to Lord Voldemort.
86. Harry Potter and Cedric Diggory.
87. She used the time-turner device which enabled her to take several classes at the same time.
88. A stag, much like his father.
89. Lavender Brown.
90. Reeter Skeeter uses her ability to turn into a beetle to sensationalise stories of students and events at Hogwarts.
91. Horace Slughorn.
92. Transfiguration.
93. Professor Quirrel.
94. *Harry Potter and the Prisoner of Azkaban.*
95. "Muggle". It is defined as "a person who possesses no magical powers…a person who lacks a particular skill or skills, or who is regarded as inferior in some way."
96. Bill, Charlie, Percy, Fred, George, Ron and Ginny.
97. An otter.
98. Albus Percival Wulfric Brian Dumbledore.
99. "Avada Kedavra", "Crucio" and "Imperio".
100. Little Hangleton. The Riddle family used to live in this area.

Chapter 2: O.W.L. Level Quiz Questions

O.W.L. Level Questions 101-115:

101. Unbelievably handsome, yet excruciatingly arrogant—Professor Lockhart turns out to be a complete fraud and walking disaster when it comes to magic. Although, he is gifted in particular when it comes to one spell, what is it?

102. Where did Harry and Cho Chang go to on Valentine's Day when they visited Hogsmeade for their date?

103. When wizards are too young to apparate or don't have access to a broom, they can travel through fireplaces instead. What is this process called?

104. Which house-elf was servant and enslaved to the Black family?

105. Who plays gamekeeper, Rubeus Hagrid in the movies?

106. Of the Death Eaters, the arrant followers of Voldemort, who is the strongest?

107. Who does Luna Lovegood end up marrying?

108. How many points does a Quidditch team receive after catching the Golden Snitch?

109. What spell is used to disarm an opponent?

110. Who is Trevor?

111. Name the orphanage that Tom Marvolo Riddle was born in?

112. Harry was accompanied to the Yule Ball, by whom?

113. What three magical objects make up the Deathly Hallows?

114. If one possesses all three objects that make up the triangle of the Deathly Hallows, what does one gain mastery over?

115.   Where do the Weasley's live?

FIND THE ANSWERS
ON THE
NEXT PAGE!

O.W.L. Level Answers 101-115

101. Memory Charms.
102. Madam Puddifoot's Tea Shop.
103. Floo Network.
104. Kreacher.
105. Robbie Coltrane.
106. Bellatrix Lestrange. She received training from the Dark Lord himself and proved a worthy accomplice to his atrocities.
107. Contrary to belief, she doesn't marry Neville Longbottom. She married Rolf Scamander, the son of Newt Scamander.
108. 150 points are scored by the team whose seeker successfully catches the Golden Snitch.
109. "Expelliarmus".
110. Trevor is Neville Longbottom's toad which he received from his great-uncle Algie as a reward for gaining entry to Hogwarts.
111. He was born on 31 December, 1926 at an orphanage named Wool's in London.
112. Parvati Patil was Harry's date for the Yule Ball, which is a tradition of the Tri-Wizard Tournament.
113. The Elder Wand, the Resurrection Stone, and the Cloak of Invisibility.
114. They can master death.
115. The Burrow.

O.W.L. Level Questions 116-130:

116.   What object do Professor Dumbledore and Harry use to view the retrieved memories of Professor Slughorn?

117.   After Ron abandons Harry and Hermione following the burden of the negative energy received from Salazar Slytherin's locket, what does he use to find his way back?

118.   Bill Weasley married who?

119.   Who replaced Cornelius Fudge as Minister of Magic?

120.   What centaur, who once lived with his colony in the Forbidden Forest later became a Professor of Divination at Hogwarts?

121.   Legend has it, that which wizard created the Cloak of Invisibility?

122.   What is a squib?

123.   The Order of the Phoenix duplicates multiple Harry's as a decoy for the real Harry using what concoction?

124.   Who do Harry, Ron and Hermione turn into in order to infiltrate the Ministry of Magic?

125.   Where does the secret passage underneath the Womping Willow lead to?

126.   What colour are Dobby's eyes?

127.   To destroy the locket of Slytherin, what did Ron use?

128.   Tonks' first name is what?

129.   What is an O.W.L.?

130.   Hogwarts students need to pass what in their seventh year in order to propel them to pursue certain careers?

FIND THE ANSWERS
ON THE
NEXT PAGE!

O.W.L. Level Answers 116-130

116. The Pensieve of Hogwarts. It is a wide and shallow dish that only the most advanced wizards dare to use.
117. The deluminator, gifted to him from Dumbledore. He could hear Hermione's voice and the device started emitting light.
118. Fleur Delacour.
119. Rufus Scrimgeour.
120. Firenze. He was banished by the other centaurs for being too friendly towards humans.
121. Ignotus Peverell, a wizard from the 13th century who did indeed evade Death by wearing it.
122. A squib is a wizard-born, they are born to at least one witch or wizard, but they possess no magical abilities.
123. Polyjuice Potion.
124. Harry impersonated Runcorn, Ron as Reg Cattermole and Hermione as Mafalda Hopkirk.
125. The Shrieking Shack, an abandoned home in the village of Hogsmeade.
126. Green
127. He used the Sword of Gryffindor after Harry spoke in parseltongue to open the locket.
128. Nymphadora.
129. An Ordinary Wizarding Level is a standardised assessment or test for firth year students at Hogwarts.
130. Nastily Exhausting Wizarding Test.

O.W.L. Level Questions 131-150:

131. What is the spell that lights the end of the casters' wand enabling them to see in the dark?

132. Whose corpse did Lord Voldemort reanimate after her murder so that he could provide Nagini another vessel in which to survive other than that of her snake embodiment?

133. What department was Professor Pomona Sprout head of at Hogwarts?

134. Who was the kind, yet rather strict matron of Hogwarts?

135. What is the name of Hermione's half-Kneazle cat?

136. The sensationalist tabloid newspaper *The Quibbler* is published and edited by whom?

137. Where is the feared fortress of Azkaban Prison located?

138. What's the name of Severus Snape's childhood home?

139. Ginny Weasley's full name is what?

140. Who does Draco Malfoy marry?

141. Why is Harry a half-blood?

142. What pirate radio station does Lee Jordan host?

143. One store located in the North side of Diagon Alley excels in selling ingredients for potion-making, what is it called?

144. What did Harry find out on his eleventh birthday?

145. Where is Hogwarts School actually located?

146. The jet black, iron-clad ball used to knock Quidditch players

off their broom is known as a what?

147.   Who was the famed, French wizard and alchemist who is recognised as the maker of the Philosopher's Stone?

148.   Nagini is based on the mythology of which country?

149.   Who foretold a prophecy of a boy who would have the power to conquer over Lord Voldemort?

150.   What is the name of the North American School of Witchcraft and Wizardry?

FIND THE ANSWERS ON THE NEXT PAGE!

O.W.L. Level Answers 131-150

131. Lumos Maxima.
132. Bathilda Bagshot.
133. Herbology.
134. Madam Pomfrey.
135. Crookshanks.
136. Xenophilius Lovegood.
137. Azkaban Prison.
138. Spinners End, Cokeworth.
139. Ginevra Molly Weasley.
140. Astoria Greengrass.
141. His maternal grandparents were muggles.
142. Potterwatch.
143. Apothecary.
144. Hagrid delivers that famous line "Harry—yer a wizard."
145. Hogwarts is slotted secretly amidst the mountainous regions of Scotland.
146. Bludger.
147. Nicholas Flamel.
148. Indonesia.
149. Sybill Trelawney.
150. Ilvermorny School of Witchcraft and Wizardry.

O.W.L. Level Questions 151-165:

151.   Who is Merope Gaunt?

152.   Salazar Slytherin was a skilled Legilimens, what exactly is this magical act?

153.   Where does Dudley Dursley go to school?

154.   In which year did Nearly Headless Nick die?

155.   What do the initials R.A.B. left on the note in Slytherin's locket stand for?

156.   Who sneaks love potion into the chocolate that Ron eats?

157.   What incantation does Professor McGonagall use to bring consciousness to the Suits of Armour in order to protect the school?

158.   Where was the lost Diadem of Ravenclaw found?

159.   Which character does Dawn French play in the movies?

160.   The headquarters of the Order of the Phoenix is situated where?

161.   Which beloved pet was killed by Death Eaters during the Battle of the Seven Potters?

162.   Ron's biggest fear is what?

163.   What does the "K" stand for in J.K. Rowling?

164.   Who did Roger Davies of Ravenclaw take to the Yule Ball?

165.   Harry's wand was made up of what?

FIND THE ANSWERS ON THE NEXT PAGE!

151. Direct descendant to Salazar Slytherin, and mother to Tom Riddle.
152. To the layman muggle this is mind-reading, but it is in fact a unique art of layered navigation through a person's mind with accurate interpretation.
153. Smeltings Academy.
154. He was executed by a failed decapitation in 1492.
155. Regulus Arcturus Black.
156. Romilda Vane.
157. "Piertotum Locomotor".
158. Voldemort hid it in the Room of Requirement believing this room was for his use only.
159. She plays the Fat Lady in *Harry Potter and the Prisoner of Azkaban*.
160. 12 Grimmauld Place in london – Sirius' family home.
161. Hedwig.
162. Spiders.
163. Kathleen.
164. Fleur Delacour.
165. It was 11" long, made of holly, and it contained a phoenix feather core.

O.W.L. Level Questions 166-180

166. What was renowned wandmaker Ollivander's first name?

167. Who was the flying instructor and Quidditch referee at Hogwarts?

168. What type of animal/bird is Buckbeak?

169. Fred Weasley lost which one of his ears?

170. Lord Voldemort ended up killing "Mad-Eye" Moody with a killing curse, but who was it initially aimed at?

171. What book did Hermione give to Harry before his first ever Quidditch match?

172. During Harry's first ever Quidditch encounter, who captained Slytherin?

173. What did Harry brew in Professor Slughorn's class that earned him a small vial as a prize?

174. Professor Slughorn presented Harry with what concoction?

175. Snape's mother married a muggle man called Tobias Snape, but what was her name?

176. Where did Lilly Potter grow up?

177. "The Boy Who Lived" was born in which village?

178. Where did Harry first encounter Professor Quirrel?

179. When did Harry first realise that he could talk to snakes?

180. There is a shapeshifter that takes the shape of the targets most feared form, what is this called?

FIND THE ANSWERS ON THE NEXT PAGE!

O.W.L. Level Answers 166-180

166. Garrick.
167. Madam Hooch.
168. Hippogriff.
169. It wasn't Fred, it was George. He lost his ear after Snape's "Sectumsempra" curse during the Battle of the Seven Potters.
170. Mundugus Fletcher.
171. Quidditch Through the Ages.
172. Marcus Flint.
173. Draught of Living Death. He did this by following the Half-Blood Prince's instructions from the textbook.
174. Felix Felicis, the bottle gave Harry twelve hours of luck.
175. Eileen Snape (née Prince).
176. Cokeworth, England.
177. Godric's Hollow.
178. Quirrel was thrilled to meet Harry when they first met at the Leaky Cauldron.
179. When he was aged 10 whilst at a zoo with his cousin Dudley.
180. Boggart.

O.W.L. Level Questions 181-200:

181. What muggle state secondary school in the United Kingdom had the Dursley's planned to send Harry to?

182. Who did Harry use the inflating charm on?

183. What broomstick did Harry own before he acquired a Firebolt?

184. Neville Longbottom's grandma gave him a gift for his first year at Hogwarts, what was the gift?

185. Which vault did Dumbledore keep the Philosopher's Stone in underneath Gringotts Wizarding Bank?

186. What spell does Harry learn from the Half-Blood Prince's textbook that he unintentionally uses to slash and cut Malfoy?

187. What is the stone-like mound taken from the stomach of a goat, that acts as an antidote to most poisons?

188. Ravenclaw's seeker position was played in by whom?

189. What enchanted writing did Dumbledore put on the snitch that he gave to Harry?

190. On which floor in the Hogwarts castle was Fluffy guarding the trap door that led to the Philosopher's Stone?

191. Who magically tampered with the rogue bludger?

192. Kingsley Shacklebolt sent what Patronus to the wedding guests at the Weasley residence?

193. What powerful charm did Remus Lupin teach Harry when he was just 13 years old?

194. How many horcruxes in total does Lord Voldemort split his soul into including himself? And what are they?

195. Which character serves a brief time as an Auror, but then goes on to become Hogwarts' Professor of Herbology?

196. After the death of Alastair Moody, who commandeered his "Mad" eye?

197. What form does Parvati Patel's boggart take?

198. How does Harry come to find the Sword of Gryffindor in the lake in the Forest of Dean?

199. Which charm is used to summon an object?

200. What symbol sits proudly on the Hufflepuff crest?

FIND THE ANSWERS
ON THE
NEXT PAGE!

O.W.L. Level Answers 181-200

181. Stonewall High.
182. Aunt Marge, who was the older sister of Vernon Dursley and was no blood relation to Harry.
183. Nimbus 2000. This was gifted to him by Professor McGonagall.
184. A Remembrall. The smoke in the ball changes colour when someone has forgotten something, but doesn't tell them what it is.
185. Vault 713.
186. "Sectumsempra".
187. Bezoar.
188. Cho Chang.
189. "I open at the close." – with reference to the snitch opening to unveil the Resurrection Stone.
190. Third floor.
191. Dobby bewitched the bludger hoping that Harry would be sent home and thereby avoid opening the Chamber of Secrets.
192. Lynx.
193. "Expecto Patronum".
194. Seven: Tom Riddle's diary, Marvolo Gaunt's ring, Salazar Slytherin's locket, Helga Hufflepuff's cup, Rowena Ravenclaw's diadem, Nagini, and Harry Potter himself.
195. Neville Longbottom.
196. Dolores Umbridge. She used it to keep track of her colleagues at the Ministry of Magic.
197. A blood-stained Mummy.
198. Snape guided Harry by conjuring a patronus for him to follow.
199. "Accio". This is one of the oldest spells known to wizard kind.
200. Badger.

Chapter 3: N.E.W.T. Level Quiz Questions

N.E.W.T. Level Questions 201-215:

201. Which first year muggle-born wizard used to follow Harry around taking his picture?

202. Where did Lord Voldemort surprisingly work after leaving Hogwarts?

203. Who was Bogrod?

204. There is a professor at Hogwarts who is a ghost, who is it?

205. What is the name of the dog that lives with Hagrid on the edge of the Forbidden Forest?

206. There is an anti-social ghost of Slytherin who Peeves is scared of, what's his name?

207. What was the first year password to the Gryffindor common room?

208. Hermione used the "Lumos Solem" spell to escape the constriction of which deadly plant?

209. Who does George Weasley marry?

210. What does a phoenix represent?

211. For how long is Harry rendered unconscious after finding the Philosopher's Stone?

212. Who turned the Tri-Wizard cup into a Portkey?

213. What are the horse-sized, skeletal creatures with leather-like black wings that pull the carriages from Hogsmeade Station to the gates of Hogwarts?

214. What is the first name of one of Voldemort's earliest Death Eaters, Macnair…?

215.   Dumbledore was born with a birthmark on his left knee, what is it?

FIND THE ANSWERS ON THE NEXT PAGE!

N.E.W.T. Level Answers 201-215

201.   Colin Creevey.
202.   Borgin and Burkes.
203.   A goblin and bank teller at Gringotts who Harry, Ron and Hermione famously put under the "Imperius" Curse to gain entry to the Lestrange Vault in stealth.
204.   Professor Cuthbert Binns, History of Magic Professor.
205.   Fang.
206.   The Bloody Baron.
207.   "Caput Draconis".
208.   Devil's Snare.
209.   Angelina Johnson.
210.   Transformation, death, and rebirth.
211.   3 days.
212.   Barty Crouch Jr.
213.   Thestrals.
214.   Walden.
215.   A map of the London Underground.

216. Which Grey Lady did the Bloody Baron kill in life?

217. Who is the owner of the dodgy pub and tavern the Hog's Head?

218. In Quidditch, what ball does Oliver Wood explain to Harry is used to score through one of the opposition's three hoops?

219. "Even in the wizarding world, hearing voices isn't a good sign." Who makes this statement?

220. What did Professor Lupin use to play his music on in class?

221. Who comes out with the hilariously classic line "Celebrity is as celebrity does, remember that."

222. Which incantation enables a caster to emit red sparks from the end of their wand?

223. Who placed the sorting hat on Harry's head during the first year?

224. Fred and George Weasley feature on the Gryffindor Quidditch team. What position do they play?

225. Following Malfoy's attempt to hex Hermione blindsided, what does "Mad-Eye" Moody do to Malfoy?

226. What spell does Hermione use to unlock the door between the trio and Fluffy?

227. What was obsessively plastered all over the collectable plates in Dolores Umbridge's office when she became Defence Against the Dark Arts teacher at Hogwarts?

228. "There were signs my slippery friend…and more than whispers." Who was Voldemort speaking to when he said

this?

229. What is the name of the root that cries when pulled from the ground?

230. What spell does Harry describe as "The wizard's bread and butter."?

FIND THE ANSWERS
ON THE
NEXT PAGE!

216.   Rowena Ravenclaw.
217.   Aberforth Dumbledore.
218.   Quaffle.
219.   Hermione.
220.   A record player.
221.   Gilderoy Lockhart.
222.   "Periculum".
223.   Professor McGonagall.
224.   Beaters.
225.   Turns him into a ferret.
226.   "Alohomora".
227.   Cats.
228.   Lucius Malfoy.
229.   Mandrake.
230.   "Stupefy". This stuns an enemy.

N.E.W.T. Level Questions 231-250:

231. There is a spell that can be casted to turn a feared boggart into something that the target finds funny. What is it?

232. Who taught the students the spell to combat boggarts?

233. Who is the werewolf who worked alongside Lord Voldemort who held visions of creating an army big enough to take over the wizarding world?

234. What is the name given to the pale green water demons who lives in the Great Lake that act viciously towards muggles and wizards alike?

235. How many staircases are there at Hogwarts?

236. Who drives the Knight Bus?

237. Dobby rescues and sets free a student from the Malfoy residence after she was caught by Death Eaters, who was it?

238. Who was appointed in charge of the Department of Magical Law Enforcement whilst it was under Voldemort's controls?

239. Who murdered Remus Lupin?

240. Which wizard was wrongly framed for the murders of Lily and James Potter?

241. How many players are there on a Quidditch team?

242. Who wrote an obituary for Dumbledore in the *Daily Prophet*?

243. What does one need to say to wipe the Marauder's Map clean?

244. Dumbledore's favourite candy is what?

245. Which fellow prefect does Percy Weasley date at school?

246. What is "Moaning Myrtle's" full name?

247. There is a statue guarding the entryway to Dumbledore's office, what is it?

248. What do Harry Potter's and Lord Voldemort's wands possess that is one of the same?

249. Who was able to turn into a dog with their Animagus abilities?

250. Who is the Master of Death?

FIND THE ANSWERS
ON THE
NEXT PAGE!

231. "Riddikulus".
232. Remus Lupin (Professor).
233. Fenryr Greyback. He was however, not a Death Eater and didn't sport the Dark Mark.
234. Grindylow. Some people have domesticated these demons.
235. 142 staircases.
236. Ernie Lee.
237. Luna Lovegood.
238. Corban Yaxley.
239. Antonin Dolohov.
240. Sirius Black.
241. Seven – three chasers, two beaters, one keeper and one seeker.
242. Elphias Doge, a Ministry of Magic jurist and special advisor to Wizengamot.
243. "Mischief Managed".
244. Lemon drops.
245. Penelope Clearwater.
246. Myrtle Elzabeth Warren.
247. Gargoyles.
248. They both share feather cores from the same wand.
249. Sirius Black.
250. Harry Potter.

N.E.W.T. Level Questions 251-265:

251. In *Harry Potter and the Goblet of Fire,* who goes to the Yule Ball with Cedric Diggory?

252. During the Quidditch World Cup, who was said to be the star player?

253. Why didn't Harry sign up for potions class in *The Half Blood Prince*?

254. Who kills Nagini?

255. In the first movie, what is Ron's final move on the monster chess board?

256. Julie Walters appears as which character throughout the movie franchise?

257. Who placed Tom Riddle's journal in Ginny Weasley's cauldron?

258. During the execution of Buckbeak, who accompanied the executioner?

259. What is the name of Nymphadora and Remus Lupin's first and only child?

260. Why did Ron attempt to curse Malfoy with?

261. During the start of the first year at Hogwarts, what house does Susan Bones get placed into?

262. In which room at Hogwarts do they hold feasts?

263. Where does Arthur Weasley work?

264. What dragon is taken from Hagrid in the first movie?

265.   Where does Vernon Dursley work and what does the company do?

FIND THE ANSWERS ON THE NEXT PAGE!

251. Cho Chang.
252. Viktor Krum.
253. He didn't score an Outstanding on his O.W.L.S.
254. Neville Longbottom.
255. Ron moved his knight to his H3 which sacrificed himself.
256. Molly Weasley.
257. Lucius Malfoy.
258. Cornelius Fudge.
259. Teddy Remus Lupin.
260. "Eat Slugs".
261. Hufflepuff.
262. The Great Hall.
263. The Ministry of Magic.
264. Norbert. He was taken as it's illegal to keep a dragon in the wizarding world.
265. Drill salesman at Grunnings.

N.E.W.T. Level Questions 266-280:

266. With the Second Wizarding War looming, who did Tonks and Lupin ask to be their son's godfather?

267. What was Neville Longbottom's biggest fear when faced with the boggart?

268. Who did Errol belong to?

269. There is a spell that can be used to remove any other magic, what is it?

270. What was the name of the Crouch family's female house-elf?

271. S.P.E.W. stands for what?

272. After mispronouncing "Diagon Alley", Harry was sent to Nocturn Alley instead. Hagrid came to his rescue from a congregation of Dark Wizards, but what was it that Hagrid was buying there?

273. Dolores Umbridge punished Harry by making him write something on a piece of paper with a magical quill, this would then painfully imprint into his hand? What did he have to write?

274. Who founded S.P.E.W. and why?

275. Ginny Weasley had a spell dating who in the sixth year?

276. As part of the decorations for Harry's seventeenth birthday celebrations, what did Hermione charm to be a gold colour?

277. Bellatrix Lestrange seemingly harbours an obsessive lust for Lord Voldemort's power, but she is actually married. What is her husband's name?

278. What is the name of the semi-human Bulgarian magical creatures who appear as young beautiful woman with pale-golden hair and skin as shiny as the moon?

279. After graduating Beauxbatons, who married Mateo Maximoff?

280. Who was the conductor of the Knight Bus?

FIND THE ANSWERS ON THE NEXT PAGE!

266.   Harry Potter.
267.   Severus Snape.
268.   The Weasley's owned Errol the Owl. He was very old and often fell flat on his face whilst delivering letters.
269.   "Finite Incantatem".
270.   Her name was Winky. She knew all the Crouch family's darkest secrets and yet she was set free by Barty Crouch Sr.
271.   The Society for the Promotion of Elfish Welfare.
272.   Flesh-Eating Slug Repellent.
273.   "I must not tell lies".
274.   Hermione Granger after what she viewed as gross injustice in the treatment of house-elves during the 1994 Quidditch World Cup.
275.   Dean Thomas.
276.   The leaves of a tree.
277.   Rodolphus Lestrange.
278.   Veela.
279.   The quarter-Veela French witch and younger sister of Fleur, Gabrielle Delacour.
280.   Stanley "Stan" Shunpike. He was eventually sent to Azkaban for being a Death Eater.

N.E.W.T. Level Questions 281-300:

281.   What house at Hogwarts did Moaning Myrtle belong to?

282.   Which dragon did Viktor Krum face in the first task of the Tri-Wizard tournament?

283.   Luna Lovegood believes in the existence of which invisible creatures that fly in through someone's ears and cause temporary confusion?

284.   What are the names of the three Peverell brothers from the tale of the Deathly Hallows?

285.   Name the Hogwarts school motto and its meaning in English?

286.   Who is Arnold?

287.   What's the address of Weasley's Wizarding Wheezes?

288.   During Quidditch try-outs, who did Ron beat to become Gryffindor's keeper?

289.   Who was the owner of the flying motorbike that Hagrid borrows to bring baby Harry to his aunt and uncle's house?

290.   During the intense encounter with the troll in the female bathroom, what spell did Ron use to save Hermione?

291.   Which wizard, who is the head of the Department for the Regulation and Control of Magical Creatures at the Ministry of Magic lost his son in 1995?

292.   When Harry, Ron and Hermione apparate away from Bill and Fleur's wedding, where do they end up?

293.   Name the spell that freezes or petrifies the body of the victim?

294. What piece did Hermione replace in the game of Giant Chess?

295. What bridge did Fenrir Greyback and a small group of Death Eaters destroy in London?

296. Who replaced Minerva McGonagall as the new Deputy Headmistress, and became the new Muggle Studies teacher at Hogwarts?

297. Where do Bill and Fleur Weasley live?

298. What epitaph did Harry carve onto Dobby's grave using Malfoy's old wand?

299. The opal neckless is a cursed Dark Object, supposedly it has taken the lives of nineteen different muggles. But who did it curse instead after a failed attempt by Malfoy to assassinate Dumbledore?

300. Who sends Harry his letter of expulsion from Hogwarts for violating the law by performing magic in front of a muggle?

FIND THE ANSWERS
ON THE
NEXT PAGE!

281. Ravenclaw. Myrtle attended Hogwarts from 1940-1943.
282. Chinese Firebolt.
283. Wrackspurts.
284. Antioch, Cadmus and Ignotus.
285. "Draco dormiens nunquam titillandus" and "Never tickle a sleeping dragon."
286. Arnold was Ginny's purple Pygmy Puff, or tiny Puffskein, bred by Fred and George.
287. Number 93, Diagon Alley.
288. Cormac McLaggen.
289. Sirius Black.
290. "Wingardium Leviosa".
291. Amos Diggory.
292. Tottenham Court Road in London.
293. "Petrificus Totalus".
294. Rook on R8.
295. The Millenium Bridge.
296. Alecto Carrow.
297. Shell Cottage, Tinworth, Cornwall.
298. "HERE LIES DOBBY, A FREE ELF."
299. Katie Bell.
300. Malfalda Hopkirk, the witch responsible for the Improper use of Magic Office.

Chapter 4: A-Z of Magical Spells, Charms & Hexes

Incantation	Classification	Outcome or Effect
Aberto	Charm	Opens up objects
Accio	Charm	Summons an object
Age Line	Enchantment	Hides stuff from younger people
Aguamenti	Charm	Shoots water from the wand
Alarte Ascendare	Spell	Shoots things high into the air
Alohomora	Charm	Opens objects that are locked
Anapneo	Spell	Clears the target's airway if choking
Anteoculatia	Hex	Turns hair from the head into antlers
Anti-Cheating	Spell	Stops cheating on exams
Aparecium	Spell	Shows invisible ink
Apparate	Spell	Teleportation Spell
Appare Vestigium	Spell	Reveals traces of recently used magic in the area
Arania Exumai	Spell	Blasts spiders away
Aqua Eructo	Spell	Shoots water from wand
Arresto Momentum	Spell	Slows objects down
Ascendio	Spell	Moves an object in an upward direction
Avada Kedavra	Curse	Murders an opponent – Unforgivable

Avenseguim	Curse	Tracking Spell
Avifors	Charm	Turns smaller objects into birds
Avis	Spell	Launches birds from the wand
—	—	—
Babbling Curse	Curse	Makes someone babble
Baubillious	Spell	Damages an opponent or creatures
Bluebell Flames	Spell	Fires blue flames at an opponent
Bombarda	Spell	Causes an explosions
Bombarda Maxima	Spell	Causes huge explosions
Bubble Head	Charm	Puts someone's head in a protective air bubble
—	—	—
Carpe Retractum	Spell	Shoots a rope from wand to grab things
Caterwauling	Charm	Detects enemies and prompts a scream
Cave Inimicum	Charm	Detects enemies and sounds an alarm
Cheering	Charm	Makes a person joyful and giddy.
Cistem Aperio	Spell	Opens stuff
Colloportus	Spell	Locks doors
Colloshoo	Spell	Causes a person's shoes to stick to the ground
Colovaria	Charm	Makes an object change colour
Confringo	Curse	Flames explode on a target
Confundus	Charm	Confuses an opponent
Conjunctivitis	Curse	Damages an enemy's

		eyesight
Cornflake Skin	Curse	Gives a person cereal skin
Crucio	Curse	Tortures an opponent – Unforgivable
Cushioning	Charm	Provides a cushion for a fall
—	—	—
Defodio	Spell	Dig out materials or objects
Deletrius	Spell	Counters "Prior Incatato"
Densaugeo	Spell	Enlarges teeth
Deprimo	Spell	Causes damage with wind
Depulso	Charm	Forces an object away
Descendo	Spell	Moves an object in a downward direction
Diffindo	Spell	Splits seams
Diminuendo	Spell	Shrinks the target to a smaller size
Dissendium	Spell	Opens a passage
Disillusionment	Charm	Makes someone blend in to the surroundings
Duro	Spell	Makes objects get hard
Drought	Charm	Dries up a puddle
—	—	—
Ears to Kumquats	Spell	Gives a person kumquat ears
Ear Shriveling	Curse	Cause a person's ears to wilt
Engorgio	Charm	Enlarges an object
Ennervate	Spell	A counter to "Stupefy"

Entrail-Expelling	Curse	Expels any entrails from a body
Episkey	Spell	Heals smaller injuries
Epoximise	Spell	Wraps objects together
Erecto	Spell	Builds stuff
Evanesco	Spell	Makes things disappear
Everte Statum	Spell	Pushes a victim backwards
Expecto Patronum	Charm	Creates a Patronus – A Defensive Guardian
Expelliarmus	Charm	Disarms an opponent
Expulso	Spell	Makes items explode
Extinguishing	Spell	Puts out fires
—	—	—
Ferula	Spell	Creates bandages
Fianto Duri	Charm	Used as a Defensive Charm
Fidelius	Charm	Masks a secret within someone
Fiendfyre	Curse	Difficult to control, a large fire curse – Dark Magic
Finestra	Spell	Turns windows to dust
Finite	Spell	Finishes spells in the area
Finite Incantatum	Spell	Cancels any current spells
Flagrante	Curse	Multiplies and burns items upon touch
Flagrate	Spell	Allows the user to write on things
Flame Freezing	Charm	Cools flames down
Flipendo	Jinx	Sends an object backwards

Flipendo Duo	Jinx	A stronger Jinx than "Flipendo"
Flying	Charm	Enables objects to fly
Fumos	Spell	A defensive cloud of smoke
Furnunculus	Curse	Produces boils on a target
—	—	—
Geminio	Spell	Replicates an object
Glisseo	Spell	Turns stairs into ramps
Gripping	Charm	Makes it easier to grip things
—	—	—
Harmonia Nectere Passus	Spell	Mends broken things
Homenum Revelio	Spell	Reveals humans who are nearby
Homonculous	Charm	Allows a wizard to track others movements on a map
Homorphus	Charm	Gilderoy Lockhart's Werewolf "cure"
Horcrux	Curse	Enables a wizard to put his soul into an object
—	—	—
Illegibilus	Spell	Makes text inelligible
Immobulus	Charm	Renders a target immobile
Impedimenta	Charm	Slows an advancing object
Imperio	Curse	Controls a person – Unforgivable
Impervius	Charm	Makes an object repel water

Incarcerous	Spell	Ties someone up
Incendio	Spell	Causes a fire
—	—	—
Lacarnum Inflamarae	Spell	Shoots a fireball from the caster's wand
Langlock	Spell	Glues target's tongue to the roof of their mouth
Legilimens	Spell	Allows the caster to read the minds of victims
Levicorpus	Spell	Hangs a victim upside down by their feet
Liberacorpus	Spell	A counter spell
Locomotor Mortis	Curse	Locks an opponent's legs together
Lumos	Spell	Creates light at the tip of the wand
Lumos Maxima	Spell	Produces a ball of light to brighten a room for a long duration of time
Lumos Solem	Spell	Creates a strong beam of light from the wand
—	—	—
Maledictus	Curse	Human can shapeshift into a snake, but they may not be able to shift back into human form
Meteolojinx Recanto	Spell	Causes weather-related spells to stop
Mimblewimble	Curse	Tongue ties it's victim
Mobiliarbus	Charm	Moves objects with the wand
Mobilicorpus	Spell	Moves unconscious bodies

Morsmorde	Spell	Conjures the Dark Mark
Muffliato	Spell	Prevents people who are close-by from listening to conversations
—	—	—
Nebulus	Spell	Creates thick fog for many blocks
Nox	Spell	A counter to "Lumos" – turns off lights
—	—	—
Oculus Reparo	Spell	Repairs eye glasses
Obliteration	Charm	Removes things like footprints
Obliviate	Charm	Erases memories
Obscuro	Spell	Blindfolds the victim
Oppugno	Spell	Makes magical items attack
Orchideous	Spell	Conjures a bunch of flowers
—	—	—
Pack	Spell	Packs a suitcase
Partis Temporus	Spell	Causes a gap to pass through in charmed barriers
Periculum	Spell	Makes fireworks from the wand tip
Permanent Sticking	Charm	Causes items to permanently stick to things
Petrificus Totalus	Spell	Binds the body
Piertotum Locomotor	Spell	Animates statues and armoured suits

Point Me	Charm	The wand acts like a compass
Portus	Charm	Makes an object a Portkey for traveling
Priori Incantatem	Spell	When brother wands duel, the loser's wand shows all spells it recently cast
Prior Incantato	Spell	Reveals a wands last spell
Protego	Charm	Cause spells to deflect back to the sender
Protego Diabolica	Charm	Creates "Black Fire" – Protective Fire
Protego Horribilis	Charm	Protects one from Dark Magic
Protego Maxima	Charm	A more powerful version of "Protego Horribilis"
Protego Totalum	Charm	Area protection spell
—	—	—
Quietus	Spell	Counter spell for "Sonorus"
—	—	—
Reducio	Spell	Returns items to their original size. Counters "Engorgio"
Reducto	Spell	Blasts solid objects aside
Relashio	Spell	Releases the user from binding
Rennervate	Spell	Cures unconsciousness
Reparo	Spell	Repairs items
Repello Muggletum	Charm	Keeps Muggles away

Repello Inimicum	Charm	Keeps evil beings away. Wide area protection
Revelio	Spell	Reveals hidden objects
Rictusempra	Charm	Tickles an opponent
Riddikulus	Spell	Use this spell to defeat a boggart by causing laughter
—	—	—
Salvio Hexia	Spell	Protection against hexes
Scourgify	Charm	A cleaning charm
Sectumsempra	Spell	Causes wounds, as if slashed by a sword
Serpensortia	Spell	Produces a snake
Silencio	Spell	Silences a victim
Slugulus Eructo	Charm	Makes an enemy vomit up slugs
Sonorus	Spell	Amplifies the voice
Specialis Revelio	Spell	Reveals hidden secrets or magical properties
Stinging Jinx	Jinx	Makes a victim feel stinging pain and get a rash
Stupefy	Spell	Knocks out an opponent
Surgito	Spell	Removes a Love Enchantment from someone
Switching Spell	Spell	Switches objects
—	—	—
Tarantallegra	Spell	Forces opponent to dance
Tergeo	Spell	Cleans up any mess
—	—	—

Unbreakable Vow	Spell	If you break the vow you make, you die
—	—	—
Ventus	Spell	Shoots a gust of hurricane force wind from the wand
Ventus Duo	Spell	Stronger than "Ventus"
Vera Verto	Spell	Turns animals into water
Verdimillious Duo	Spell	More powerful than "Verdimillious"
Vipera Evanesca	Spell	Makes snakes vanish
—	—	—
Vulnera Sanentur	Spell	Heals victims
—	—	—
Waddiwasi	Spell	Unsticks an object
Wingardium Leviosa	Charm	Makes on object fly

Also, in the series…

Don't miss out on the #1 New Release and Part Two in the series: *Harry Potter Facts For Muggles.*

One Last Thing

If you have enjoyed this book, please don't forget to write a **review** of this publication. It is really useful feedback as well as providing untold encouragement to the author.

Printed in Great Britain
by Amazon